The Last Lamb

A Journey Home

Carol Watson

To Doris,
Thank you for being so
special! Stand strong! Always.
Carol Watson

Dedicated to parents everywhere whose children such as these:

Theresa Gerome

Peggy Parsh

Thomas Watson

Anne Holman

Barry Lehr

Mark Kiper

Terrance Dempsey, Jr.

Julian Hedayatnia

Matthew Schellenberger

. . . have been called home early.

I

❀

The sheep were gone. Slain and stolen. The old shepherd sank to his knees, wailing in the wind. Tending flock had been his life and it had just been taken from him. Thieves at midnight, out to make underhanded sales in lamb's blood for Jerusalem's Passover, crept up the hillside and with deadly darts brought the sheep down one at a time.

Lonely bleating in the bushes followed the robbers as they dragged dead carcasses to waiting wagons. Blood trickled down the wheels as the creaking load slipped eerily into the silent night heading for the temples.

The shepherd rose from an anguished position. Gnarled fingers clenched and extended around his staff as if undecided what to do next, where to go in the darkness. Looking into the wind, a desert cloud ladened with sand hit him with force. Wrapping a tangled blanket about his leathered face, Abijah bowed low against the sand's sting. With swaying lantern, tugging his small donkey, the shepherd searched for the only lamb left behind, an aging ewe about to give birth. Somewhere she was in the thicket. Abijah climbed among blackened briars searching. Tears stung his eyes and brambles tore his skin.

"Maia," he called into bushes that slapped back at him. A rustling sound and whimpered baaing drew him to a nesting cove, a den encircled by thistles and thorns.

On hands and knees, the old man crawled into the snug alcove, away from the sting of the storm. He drew his arm around the sweat of the heaving mother. Laying his white beard into the comforting wool, he clung to her like a lost child.

"Maia, good little mother. You have born me many lambs, and now they have been taken from us, their blood to be washed across doorways. Push dear one. This is our last."

The night wind pounded its fist outside the enclosure as the beast bore her lamb. With a final sigh of love to her master, Maia closed her eyes and died.

6

II

The sun spewed its hot breath as Abijah hobbled his way into Jerusalem. Shouting vendors cursed, sheep bleated, and pigs squealed. The poor cried for bread. The old donkey, head down, hair matted, and eyes half closed, followed the slow footsteps of the shepherd. Under the old man's robe, tucked warmly to his breast, was the new-born lamb. Abijah's heart cradled the new life as if the strength of movement might give life to his brittle bones.

He had nowhere to go, nowhere to stay. Now that his flock was gone, he came into the city looking for milk to nurture the young one. He couldn't do the things that nature automatically handled concerning babies. His ewes always did the job of feeding, nurturing, and cleaning. Abijah's only hope in saving this lamb would be to find another ewe from the marketplace willing to take over the job of motherhood. The thought of this last lamb living a fruitful life beyond his own was the only hope nudging Abijah on.

Winding his way aimlessly without direction, he passed through old gates into an avenue that led to the Roman market. Civic buildings, white and rose misted marble, rose like flesh around him. Statues of gods and humans guarded portals of every building and street. It seemed the Romans had a god for every day of every week. Scarcely a month went by they didn't celebrate a holiday in honor of a god. Abijah, with his Jewish upbringing thought, *"Thou shalt have no other Gods before me."* However, he fought back the opposing thought whispering, *"But where was God when the thieves came?"*

As a young mystic and dreamer of the scriptures, Abijah related best to God in nature. For this reason, the shepherd's life was in Abijah's blood. He loved the freedom of the open fields and sleeping under stars in makeshift shelters. He was by nature a vagabond roaming the grassy hillsides with the unconditional love of his flock and their dependence upon his care.

Other shepherds came to the fields every day

from their homes and families. But ever since he lost his young wife, Hedia, years ago in a violent sandstorm, Abijah left the domestic existence. Instead he chose the nomad life, roaming the fields with his herds.

Childless and alone, Abijah's flock became his family. He named them, pampered them, talked to them, led them, and loved them like his own children. Shepherding had been a profitable existence. The wool brought in enough money for him to live contentedly. As Abijah steadily grew older, and his eyes dimmed, it got harder to watch over his flock.

Now everything had changed. To the marketplace he once considered life, fun, and celebration, he now returned old, afraid, and alone. He wandered like a beggar without direction, and without hope.

III

✿

Abijah moved aside to a dried brick wall as boots from a battalion of soldiers clicked precisely past him, almost tripping upon an old woman cleaning turnips in her doorway. The woman's bones creaked as she lowered herself to lift a basket. Abijah looked down at her blankly.

"I could use that donkey." She said, grinning toothlessly.

"I could use some of that goat's milk," he replied, eyeing a gourd jug on the ground.

To her surprise, Abijah moved his donkey forward as if it didn't really matter what he did. He nodded mumbling, "I'll load your turnips."

Mechanically he pulled the lamb from his coat,

and handed it to her while he began hooking her flimsy baskets to the side of his donkey.

Mouth agape, standing speechless, the old woman lowered her eyes, and looked into the face of the newborn lamb. "Oh my!" she whispered, "What a sweet blessing."

She felt the little lamb's heart pounding against her own. Dipping her fingers into the jug, then slipping them into the pink mouth, the lamb hungrily suckled the nourishment. When the little one was set on the ground, he squatted unabashedly to leave a trickle of water. The old woman smiled a sunbeam, crinkling her face like a desert dried raisin.

Studying Abijah she asked, "So! Why have I the honor of your help?"

Abijah, as if to work off some inner anger, continued to load the turnips. "I don't really know," he said, "I've met with some bad luck, and I have nothing else to do. I'm headed for the market anyway."

He pulled the old donkey forward, and nodded for the old woman to join him. Nuzzling the lamb, she hobbled along next to the two baskets of turnips bumping on the flanks of the bony donkey.

"What's your name?" she asked.

"Abijah, What is yours?"

"Rachel, but most of the neighbors just call

me Turnip Lady because I like to root around into everyone's business."

Rachel laughed at what she thought was funny. Abijah couldn't help but smile back.

"Have you heard?" she said, "The soldiers have just caught Barabbas, the chief of rebels. He's to be crucified today."

Abijah stopped abruptly and turned to face her. "You mean the most notorious rebel in Rome?"

He thought back to the nights on the hillsides when bands of rebels and zealots gathered in caves refusing surrender to the dominions of Roman tyranny. They ambushed Roman caravans, stripped the camels and donkeys, stole anything hauled for Rome, and eliminated leaders. What criminal could equal Barabbas?

Emperor Caesar Tiberius of Rome ruled Judea. He was honored not only as an emperor, but also as a god. In Jerusalem, a district of Judea, Pontius Pilate governed Judea in the name of Caesar. He ruled his territory with the precision of a military leader.

Any revolutionists or criminals defying the authority of the Roman Empire were put to death through crucifixion. It was a gruesome public display. It warned anyone of questioning the authority of the Roman Empire. In Jerusalem, no one could send a man to death except Pontius Pilate.

Normally it was not custom to execute on a

Jewish Holiday. Today and tomorrow the Jews would celebrate their historical release from the land of Egypt. The old story was told and retold in every household. How an angel of death, sent from the Lord, had swooped low over every house in the land of Egypt, gathering to himself the first-born of every generation of both man and beast, from the son in the deepest dungeon to the servant of the palace. Only those homes where the blood of a lamb had been sprinkled escaped the sudden slaughter.

Actually, the Jews were celebrating the feast of freedom from Pharaoh while under bondage to Caesar, who was worse than Pharaoh. In a concerned tone Abijah leaned toward Rachel, "No crucifixion can or would take place over our holy holiday."

She replied, "I heard that Barabbas is such a big catch that they are going to have him done in as soon as possible. That means immediately. Passover or no Passover. They are going to get around it by honoring the old Jewish tradition of releasing another prisoner to the public. In order to do this they have arrested three other criminals along with Barabbas. They know that the local Romans want Barabbas' head, so they figure the release of one of the other criminals will pacify the Jewish community during their holiday."

Irritated, Abijah wheeled forward, staff in

13

hand, tugging at the donkey's halter leading past the ugliest and dirtiest tenement districts. They shoved their way through the area of lavish Roman baths, and past the gymnasium to the Damascus Gate. They crossed the line of ancient walls, leading through the gate to the new Roman market. They stopped. Ahead gathered a shouting crowd.

IV

❁

The woman, Mary, breathlessly slipped through the angry mob. Her small sandaled feet, brown with red dust, wove among the jackals of shouters. Her white mantle floated about her gray-streaked hair as if she was spreading wings. News had flashed quickly through her village that Jesus, her son, had been arrested the previous evening at midnight in the Garden of Gethsemane, outside the Eastern Gate.

All along she had known this day was coming. It had been prophesied. Even foretold in her heart. Her spiritual side was prepared, but her human side felt the knot of fear tightening in her stomach.

Word of Jesus' popularity had begun as a

gentle rain that turned into a storm. Gossip began from Galilee to Samaria and from Perea beyond the Jordan River. Many sang his praises. From blind men who crawled to him, to sick men who placed themselves at His feet. He healed, preached, and walked with the lowly, the unloved, and the lavished. He spread messages of liberating grace, hope for the sinful, and encouragement to the weary. He touched lives with faith, the simple faith that anyone could understand.

"Behold Him! Our Messiah!" the crowds hailed.

But others howled against Him for He spoke against the temple and made Himself one with God. Rome had no legitimate quarrel with Jesus, except that He sought recruits, this always being a threat to the Empire. Jesus' greatest enemies were the priests and the scribes. They charged Him with teaching blasphemy and errors of the church.

It was these priests and scribes that frightened Mary today. They were everywhere in the marketplace wagging their beards and planning among themselves saying, "Stone the Nazarene! Kill Him!"

Heart pounding in her chest, Mary lifted her eyes to where she knew her son would be, displayed to the crowds from the marble porch of Pilate's fortress.

The great door thudded closed as four beaten

prisoners were brought forth by guards armed with whips. Jesus was among them. He was blood splattered, whip marked, and wore a crown of thorns upon His head. His strong but sorrowful gaze scanned the crowd.

Mary's knuckles whitened as she wailed inwardly, *"My son. My dear child."*

A high-ranking officer with a brushlike plume on his helmet stepped forward. Giving an order to the guards, they shoved each prisoner forward to the edge of the porch for all to clearly see. The crowd hushed as the officer raised his hand. His eyes pierced the crowd as he shouted,

"Which man should Pilot release for the Passover? Barabbas, the Nazarene, or one of the two thieves?"

When Mary heard the name Barabbas, she sucked in her breath with hope. Someone in the crowd shouted, "Barabbas eats vipers for breakfast!" Everyone laughed.

A crowd of priests and scribes, black robes mingling like hawk's wings, edged forward into the sunlight. From behind them spread out a tattered group of ruffians.

A woman with unruly hair yelled, "Free the Nazarene!"

A man under a canopy, cupping his mouth hollered, "Let the Nazarene go!"

Slowly people began chiding in one at a time,

17

here and there, "The Nazarene, the Nazarene!" Even Mary, hands to her breast, began an unconscious prayer with the name.

Suddenly, as if on signal, a pulsing name rose in unison from every corner of the market place. It began in a low rhythm and crescendoed to a raucous pulsing uproar, "Barabbas! Barabbas! Barabbas!"

The officer turned, surprised as were many in the crowd, and tried to hush the rebellion. The legion had not expected this. But the shouting continued without interruption.

Finally after consulting with two other officers, the soldiers waved the crowd to silence. Reluctantly the officers stepped forward, growling like jackals deprived of a kill. The captain of the guards stepped forward as two trumpeters blasted attention for the final decision.

"Let it be known that Rome, in honor of the Jewish Passover, will release . . ." (And here he hesitated a moment scowling at the man he grabbed and shoved forward toward the crowd), "Barabbas!" A dissonant cheer arose.

Mary gave a faint cry, turned and ran, pushing her way past two grinning Pharisees, who rubbed their hands in evident approval.

"*No*!" she moaned.

Running blindly past blurred faces, someone caught her in comforting arms. Her face fell gently into the warm woolly grace of the newborn lamb, and her tears brushed against the tender innocent eyes. The smell, the feel, and the softness embraced her with balm. Lifting her head, she recognized her friend, the Turnip Lady. It was Joseph's mother, Rachel.

V

❀

Rachel placed the small lamb into Mary's arms, knowing well the feeling of loss. Having been her mother-in law, neighbor, and friend for many years, the two women's eyes met in shared pain in losing a loved one. Joseph had been Rachel's dearest son, and the love and life of Mary's heart. Sadly he had been laid to rest many years ago. Both women had reconciled their grief, moving on in the adjustment. Now this crucifixion of Jesus loomed over Mary the Mother, and Rachel the grandmother.

Mary collected herself enough to speak, "This hidden sorrow I have always known, but could never identify has arrived. It has lived with me ever since Simeon the blind man spoke of it at

Jesus' birth dedication in the courtyard of the temple long ago. He prophesied to me saying, 'Yea, a sword shall pierce through thy own soul.' I have lived with his words all these years."

"Oh, Rachel, I will need your comfort in the days to come."

As the two women embraced, Mary searched her mother-in law's eyes for the loving wisdom that would give her strength. Tears welling up, Mary took the lamb, pulling it closer to her, and prayerfully closed her eyes in silent supplication.

Abijah stood transfixed in stunned silence staring at Mary. He had never forgotten that glowing composure after all these years. Even the fine lines of time hadn't tempered the face that etched in it a countenance of strength and assurance.

"Mary?" Abijah spoke softly, "Do you remember me?"

Mary turned toward the old man, looking puzzled as she studied his leathered face. He answered, "I was one of the shepherds long ago that visited you and Joseph that holy night in the stable in Bethlehem."

With these words, Mary's memory moved back in time when the angels were singing, when the light of the star was bathing her newborn, and when the shepherds and kings were in adoration of her child. It occurred to Mary now that even back then as she pondered in her heart all the things that were happening to her, she knew intuitively that this day of separation would come. She held herself for a brief moment in the past savoring the relief of the moment.

She remembered there was one young shepherd in particular that she and Joseph had especially liked. He had returned alone and unexpectedly that chilly evening bringing locks of wool from sheep of the pastures tucking a blanket of warmth around the sleeping Child. This young man, Abijah, was mourning the loss of his wife. He returned the next few nights to seek counsel with Joseph. With sheep grazing upon the hillsides, Joseph and Abijah sat out under the stars and talked.

Mary pulled herself back to reality focusing on Abijah.

"I see you still have the shepherd staff that Joseph carved for you." She wistfully touched the beautiful cedar carvings, "Are you still shepherding?"

"Well," Abijah's eyes lowered, he spoke low, "I've just lost everything."

Mary said, " I'm sorry to hear this. We are both at a loss right now, but nevertheless, it is good seeing you again, Abijah."

VI

Suddenly startled by the sound of horses pounding the pavement, Abijah propelled both women out of the pathway of hooves striking sparks on the cobblestone street. Like weevils in a grain bin, the ugly temperament of the soldiers snarled at those they nearly trampled.

"Please stay with me," cried Mary, "I have to meet the others. Hurry!"

Still clutching the lamb with Abijah jerking his donkey to follow, and Rachel hurrying behind, Mary pushed her way through the crowd that gathered along the road. Weaving into the sea of bodies, they hurried past the bulky shadow of the Roman barracks. A burly officer, smelling of sweat and wine, was clearing the street yelling, "Make way, clear the road. We can't let the crosses rest on a holiday!"

Another officer on a white horse, stepping in time to the beat of a lone drum, held an insignia aloft with solemnity and arrogance. The plume of his helmet curved like a blackbird's wing over his head and down his neck. His cloak was a blotch of scarlet against the dusty street.

Mary looked along the countless holiday booths of willow branches and awnings lining the street. Air reverberated with the coaxing of hustlers and the bawling and blatting of camels and sheep. Soldiers were screaming orders and shoving aside vendors. News of the crucifixion had spread like a disease. People, curious onlookers, always paraded into town mile after mile on the highways from Judea to Caesarea on the coast of the Great Sea and east from the ancient city of Damascus.

From out of nowhere rang the name, "Mary!" Looking around, she spied her friends, John and Mary Magdalene. After quick embraces and introduction of Abijah, the concerned group was pushed aside by a flank of soldiers shouting, "Make way for the death procession!"

VII

John, Mary Magdalene, and Rachel moved close to Mary, enclosing her in support. Abijah, still reeling from the enormity of the moment and the realization of what was about to happen, rallied to the conviction that his problems had become minute. He remembered that Jesus, a Babe he visited long ago in a manger, was born the Son of God. He remembered the glory, the blinding light, and the great host of angels singing, still awestruck at the memory. Yet at this moment that Child, now grown to a Man, was to be crucified on a cross. His knees weakened and he looked to the skies for Jehovah's wrath.

The clouds, veiled in a dark shroud, blew down chilly winds. Abijah pulled his old donkey closer for protection, laying a comforting hand upon Mary's arm. The five waited, hardly daring to breathe.

Each to be crucified bore his own cross, dragging it in a trail of dust. They had been beaten, bruised, and their beards yanked out. Four guards accompanied each prisoner. One in front, one behind, and one on both sides. All carried whips. Keepers in the gate towers blew trumpets to clear the portals and let the procession through.

Jesus, followed by weeping women, was bending under the weight of His beam. The crown of thorns, blood coated, bit into His brow displaying a mockery to His Kingship. As He passed Mary His sandal broke and He stumbled upon it, falling to the ground. His garment showed stains of blood around the shoulders, revealing patches of raw flesh showing through. It was unusual for scourged men to be crucified. Scourging generally preceded release, a warning to mend the ways. But today was different.

Jesus' bruised lips moved. Loud and commanding, His voice rang out, "Weep not for Me, but weep for yourselves and for your children. For if they do this while I am yet with thee, what will they do when I am no longer at hand?"

The crowd surged forward to help but the

whips rose, forcing the people back slowly. Jesus paused a moment in the dust to raise His sorrowful gaze, sensing His mother. She stepped forward still clutching the lamb.

Jesus' and Mary's eyes met. For a moment time stopped. The Omnipotent God had joined them in this communion of souls. The Master and the mother, receiving a jewel of all knowing, and a precious moment of sanctified love.

Jesus, the Son of God, would willfully and obediently cross over the wall of death, unafraid and triumphant. He would become the God symbol showing that there was absolutely nothing in life to fear, not even death. Jesus knew He would be taking the greatest journey ever in the experiences of man. For He knew He would not only cross over, but He would rise and return physically to earth again to prove resurrection and God's love for all mankind. Thereby demonstrating the greatest faith ever to exist on earth.

Mary would be left to set an example of her love for God, by giving back her child at the difficult time when God calls them home. Whether a child stays three, fourteen, or in Jesus' case, thirty three years, all are His children, and all from earth must return, thus completeing the missions or lessons learned. In this role of bereavement, and in willfully giving back to God what is His, *under any conditions of departure*, Mary would demonstrate the greatest parental love and faith. Her eyes penetrated the darkness and the sorrow to come, piercing into her son's soul.

"Shalom my dear child."

He forced a tiny hint of a smile. *"You know me well. My spirit is not afraid. My body will die, but My soul will go with great joy back to My Father. Shalom mother. I am with you always."*

Jesus' eyes lowered to the lamb in Mary's arms. She shared a smile with Him as they both remembered the sunny days on the hillsides, romping with the newborn lambs. As a young boy Jesus loved to remind His mother that the lamb symbolized the Kingdom of God. "Lambs are animals of fear," He would say. "They need a shepherd for love, protection, and guidance. Just as we need God." It became a fun conversation between them.

Mary would always tease, "I know Jesus, you tell me these things many times."

Jesus would laugh and say, "I just want to make sure you need never be afraid."

Mary would laugh in response, "When I am afraid, Jesus, I will let you know." She would hug him, tousle his silky brown hair and treasure this bond they had until He would be off chasing lambs again.

A heavy whip cracked upon Jesus' shoulders. Mary jumped back. Jesus struggled to His feet and continued dragging the cross through the crowd.

VIII

"You! Shepherd Man! Yes, you with the staff! Is that your lamb?"

Abijah nodded. An officer pushed forward with his eyes riveted upon the lamb in Mary's arms. He carried a mallet in a leather pouch that hung over his shoulders. Spitting between yellowed teeth he bellowed, "Pilate has been screaming for a lamb to sacrifice. Shepherd, take that animal to the Fortress Antonia. This gold coin will get you in the front gate. He thrust it into Abijah's palm. Present it in the palace quarters. Pilate is an impatient man so get a move on you! This is an order!"

Abijah lowered his head without questioning and took the lamb from Mary, her face ashen. He glanced up toward the balcony and porches of the fortress. Then as fast as his old legs could carry him, he hobbled down the crooked sunless street toward the marble steps. Aching joints brought him to the top porch. There he presented the coin to a soldier who hurriedly escorted him through bronze portals, past door porters, and down carpeted corridors.

Catching his breath, he stopped under the swords of guards. They knew the situation, and hurriedly pushed Abijah between heavy brocaded curtains to a wide mosaic chamber. Abijah's knees were shaking. He found himself in the private bedchamber of Pilate.

Pilate, his fat belly protruding under a short tunic, lay upon pillows on a canopy bed. He didn't notice Abijah blending into the corner curtains. This Governor of Judea, after turning Jesus over to the High Priest Caiaphas to be crucified, had felt great pangs of conscience so severe that he was becoming delirious.

"My hands are covered with blood!" he screamed. "Bring me the basin."

A chambermaid appeared.

Abijah watched in fascination and fear as Pilate washed and rewashed his hands in ashes, water, and oil. He kept mumbling, "If I sacrifice a lamb, God may forgive me." Abijah stepped back into the shadows of the curtain.

Next to the bedchamber was an adjacent room. From out of its beaded doorway appeared Procula, Pilate's wife. She was as stricken as her husband. Her black hair stormed around her in a wild cascade of fury. She was tense, rubbing her bony hands up and down her soft silk gown.

"I warned you! Oh Pilate! I warned you! Why didn't you face up to the Pharisees? This is nothing but a religious quarrel. I told you of my dream. It was a message to save you from this infamy. Have nothing to do with the just man from Nazareth. Oh! I warned you! And you didn't listen to me."

Pilate, eyes raving wild, looked past her shouting, "I tried! In your Jehovah's name I tried! I released Him, sending Him to Herod in Galilee, and they sent Him back to me. I planned on turning Jesus loose with the Jewish Passover. But something went wrong! It went wrong! I wash my hands of this deed woman."

Pilate quivered, reached to the basin, and washed his hands again. Getting up out of bed he pushed his way past his wife and slumped down into an ornate chair, his nails scratching the armrests etched with black snakes. Scratching. Scratching. He stared forward unfocused for some time.

The lamb, as if lost in this perfumed, stuffy place, wiggled in Abijah's arms and let out a small baahing cry. Suddenly Pilate jumped up and cried out, "The lamb! Where is the lamb! I must make a sacrifice to cleanse myself of this deed."

Frightened, Abijah stepped out of the shadows. Pilate's eyes dilated as he stared at the lamb before him. Jumping up, running over to a desk, he opened a drawer and pulled out a pearl-handled knife. Pilate grabbed at the lamb's throat to slit it. Something snapped inside Abijah, giving him strength and overcoming his age. He yanked away, still holding the lamb, bellowing a full-mouthed defense.

"Nooooo! Not this one! This is my last lamb!"

Pilate moved back startled. As he regained himself to go after Abijah and the lamb again, Procula jumped between them, planting herself squarely in front of her husband. Her fury was unleashed. "Pilate! Stop this! My dream, the one in this very bed, was about the blood of the lamb. Don't stain it with more blood upon your hands. Don't kill this one!"

Pilate blinked, ran an arm across his sweating beard, and staggered back to his basin. He began washing his hands again.

Procula turned viciously to Abijah and hissed, "Get out of here! Leave Pilate to me!"

Abijah quickly fled the palace.

IX

⊛

Lost in the sea of holiday hecklers, shouting vendors, and the laughter and chatting of magpie women, Abijah moved quickly through the streets. Grotesque shadows were beginning to cover the city like giant thousand-legged worms. He looked up to the Northeast to the snow covered Mt. Hermon. It sat like a king lording over the hills of Judea.

Where was the procession? Where were Mary, Rachel, John, and Mary Magdalene? He wanted to be with them. He wanted to see. He wanted to be a part of whatever was going to happen. He knew God wouldn't let His Son be crucified and there would be some kind of divine intervention. He didn't want to miss this! He also needed to find his donkey that he left with John.

In the distance, a craggy hill thrust its shoulders against the sky. This was the hill known as Golgatha where crosses stood. They were as much of Rome as the roads, the ships, the pagan gods, and the aqueducts.

Abijah, breathing hard, followed a crowded thin and uneven line of spectators. They were leaving the highway and winding a torturous way up a narrow dirt road leading up to the crucifixion hill.

Halfway up the hill and unable to carry the lamb any farther, Abijah chose a rocky promontory to rest upon. Placing the lamb down, the young one stretched its legs, scampered around, and pounced upon a lonely hawk feather stuck in the sand. Sniffing and then sneezing, leaving a soiled spot, it finally folded up into a pile of grass and went to sleep.

Abijah never tired of watching the playfulness and exhilaration of life in lambs. Pouncing, hopping, climbing, running, and rolling. He thought of them as cherubs wearing curly coats and little black shoes.

A ray of sunshine poked through a dark cloud shining its light upon the small sleeping one, the shepherd sensing that God had stretched forth His Hand to caress the innocence and wonderment of this new creation. It was such a contrast to the dark lonely crosses in the distance.

Abijah knew the soldiers would be taking a

short break before the scheduled hour, so he too lay back tucking his arms behind his head to rest. Winds blew across his bearded face, gently stroking his mind into sleep.

It was these same winds that cut caves in the face of the sandstone cliffs Abijah napped upon. These punctures of caves looked like lifeless sockets. The foot of the cliff, stones fallen away, left a wide opening resembling the toothless grin of a skull. The skull-like qualities of the cliff gave it its name, Golgatha meaning, "place of the skull."

A few feet away deep inside one of the lifeless sockets hidden into the bowels of darkness crouched Barabbas. He had fled for his life after being released, only to choose this place, a place where he could follow the activities of the thieves to be crucified.

A young man with dark eyes, a bronze build, and a commanding voice, Barabbas rarely allowed others to get too close to him. Leader and most notorious bandit of the Roman Empire, he lay stunned at the day's outcome. Ready to go out in a blaze of glory, to die for freedom and the cause, he now found himself released and hunted down again.

This unexpected dismissal humiliated him. Mixed emotions ran through his idealistic mind. He prided himself on being the goader of Rome. He was leader of men, of ideas, and of revolutionary courage. But today someone overruled him. Was this someone more of a threat to the Empire than he, the great Barabbas? This other was a Nazarene. His name was Jesus. *Am I envious? This is crazy! Where did He come from? I overheard others saying that He was a King of some sort. Why have I not been informed of this man?* Both perplexity and fascination held Barabbas captive as he rubbed his bruised and bloody face. He strained to see through swollen and blood crusted eyelids toward the light. Watching.

Suddenly against the cave light a figure appeared. A low sparrow warble was heard. Barabbas answered the trill in the same manner, fingers in teeth.

"Barabbas! Is that you?" a young voice whispered into the silence of the cave.

"Yes! Did you bring the supplies?"

A young boy appeared in the mouth of the cave.

"I brought goat cheese, a flask of wine, a dagger, and the clothing."

"Good boy, Elrad. Did you check to make sure you weren't followed?"

"Yes Barabbas."

Barabbas crawled out from the shadows. The boy clamored over rocks, coming into the cave entrance calling, "Barabbas, look what I found outside the cave. It's a baby lamb. It was wander-

36

ing around looking lost. He's followed me in and must think that I'm his mother. Isn't he cute?"

The lamb followed on wobbly legs, wagging his tail, stumbling into the shadows, reaching his pink nose up into the broken bones of Barabbas' hand. The warmth of the little tongue licked the whip wounds on the palms, unfolding the big man's heart.

For a few moments he was lost in his childhood and the lambs he raised with his father, brothers, uncles and cousins. There was pungent smelling hay, the feel of lamb's warm breath against his cheek, the taste of sweet mother's milk, and the glow of fellowship among men. He missed these times and the simplicity of life then.

Suddenly jarred from his reflections, someone called into the cave. Barabbas quickly grabbed Elrad off the ground and flattened them both against the stone wall next to the entrance. There was no time to hide. A shadow of a man entered the opening calling,

"Little one. Where are y . . ."

Quietly setting down the boy, and with the speed of the great fighter he was, Barrabbas assailed Abijah from behind, jerking his powerful arm up into his neck, holding a dagger to his throat, immobilizing the old man.

"Sorry friend. This cave is taken," growled Barabbas.

Abijah's heart fluttered, his stomach tightened, and he couldn't catch his breath. He dizzied and slumped forward hanging into Barabbas' arms.

Barabbas dragged Abijah to a rock platform and laid him down. Grabbing the wine flask from Elrad and pouring droplets into the unconscious man's mouth, he slapped his cheeks a few times. Abijah's eyes fluttered opened and he slowly sat up. Spying the lamb at Barabbas' feet, he blinked awake. Remembering the moment, he glared at the attacker.

"Who are you?" he sputtered.

"I apologize for scaring you. I thought you might be a soldier or bounty hunter following my nephew and me."

Abijah studied the strong jaw line, bearded with sweat and blood, raw whip marks upon the muscular neck and chest, with only a loincloth barely covering the bruised thighs.

"Why . . . aren't you . . . aren't you Bar . . (He could hardly say the name) Barabbas?"

Barabbas squared his six foot frame, taking a step back. His voice was resonant and baritone.

"Yes, I'm Barabbas. You know of me?"

Abijah took hold of his staff, pushing on it to stand. He spoke low and looked Barabbas squarely in the eye.

"I've been watching your men comb these hill-sides for years. You have never harmed the commoner. In fact I have been impressed with your helping the poor. Up until lately, I have supported your cause for freedom from Pilate's tyranny. I'm not sure now. Two nights ago my entire herd was killed and carted off by rogues of the night. I have nothing left but this lamb and a donkey. Were those your men who slain my herd?"

Barabbas narrowed his brows, clenched his fists, kicking the dust with his bloody foot. Turning to Abijah, his composure of kindness vanished and he spoke like the leader of bandits. He spit into the dirt before speaking.

"They joke about me eating vipers for breakfast. But I tell you this on my honor of Jehovah. I would pick the bones of those serpents of scum if I could. Caesar sets his regiments of ruffians to disguise themselves as my men, coming to the hills to waylay our cause in any way they can to make us look bad. Women and young girls are raped, murdered, and left for the vultures in the desert. Goods of the decent are stolen and ransacked. Then the Empire decrees these acts of violence are from Barabbas. I'm the scapegoat for Rome's folly. My notoriety gets bigger each day. I will spend the rest of my days fighting the tyranny of Caesar. No friend, those were not my men. But I certainly would like to get my fingers around their throats."

Abijah nodded thoughtfully and introduced himself, then asked Barabbas why he was hiding in the caves and not escaping the city. Barabbas cleared his throat asking,

"Abijah, can I count on your help if I explain?"

"Go ahead," answered the shepherd.

Barabbas leaned against a jagged rock, pointing a finger in the direction of the crosses, lowering his voice but speaking very distinctly, "Rome doesn't know this, and we are trying to keep it quiet, but the other thief to be crucified is my brother, Tivon. He hasn't been with my revolution for some time because he left to help my ailing mother in Capernaum after my father died. While there, He fell in love with Shera. They married and had a son, Elrad here. Elrad is the center of Tivon's life. My brother is a kind and gentle man, always laughing, always helping everyone. He never had the stomach for fighting.

"Yesterday the Romans caught him moving aside a marble statue that fell off one of their temple porches. It was blocking the road. They accused him of trying to steal it. The soldiers had been drinking and beat my brother past recognition. Now he is being crucified as a thief. This type of Roman justice is what I have been fighting against. I can understand Rome's quarrel with me, but not my brother!

"We want to rescue Tivon from his crucifixion. I'm doing it especially for Elrad's sake. This boy is like my own son. I am not married and have no family. Tivon is the caretaker for my mother, his wife, and child. What kind of a man would I be if I didn't try to save my family?

"My men have been alerted as to what to do. We'll give it our best. Won't we Elrad? (He gave the boy, whose lower tip trembled, a bear hug.) I have a plan. Are you with us Abijah?"

Abijah figured he had nothing to lose at this point in his life, so he stuck our his hand. As the two men locked wrists, trumpets blasted from the hillside. Barabbas turned abruptly, downing the rest of the wine, smashing the flagon into the rocks, wiping his arm across his wet beard, and stuffing the goat cheese into his mouth.

"Quickly Elrad, give me the clothing you brought."

X

❀

As the sun rose high over the city walls, guards noticed an old shepherd, a boy leading a lamb, and a hooded priest, walking toward the crucifixion arena. The priest's shadowed face was covered and bowed in prayer. His clasped hands were covered by the flowing sleeves of the braided robe that draped into the dust. The soldiers were busy gossiping about the big news of the day. A graveled voice said,

"Never in a million years would Pilate have let Barabbas go. Rome could have no greater enemy. What happened? Someone has made a grievous mistake. I would hate to be in the shoes of the release officer that addressed that raucous crowd, giving Barabbas up."

Another soldier interrupted, punching the first in the arm. "If Barabbas was crucified, then who would we blame for our parties?"

Laughter and clinking of metal cups followed a scuffle of moving a wagon loaded with gravel ready to fill the holes, securing the crosses once they were raised.

In some ways the crucifixion was more exciting than the Roman Circus or the gladiator fights because it took longer to die. The crowd could participate to a certain degree with petty torments, jeers, and mockeries. To shorten the suffering, if chosen, the soldiers would break the legs of the crucified, to collapse the lungs faster. In some cases they just ran a sword through the prisoner's side. In most cases the crowd could control the length of time it took to take a victim by badgering the officers. This form of entertainment was a place of confusion, a place where people enjoyed killing. The smell of death brought vultures dancing in the winds high above this hill of crosses.

Boulders that were cleared from the hilltop formed a crude amphitheater at one end of the arena. Usually the audience was made up of women and town rubble. But today there were Pharisees and Sadducees from the Sanhedrin, the ruling court of Jewish religious and civil affairs. Priests were in linen robes while Pharisees were identified by the blue fringe about the skirts. Most of them stood together rubbing their hands, raising insults before the show:

"Where are the miracles now?"

"He saved others, but he can't save himself."

The prisoners had been stripped of all clothing except for the loincloths. Robes, tunics, and sandals were tossed aside and piled upon a makeshift table of an old door. These would be divided among the soldiers. The guards were arguing over the purple robe of Jesus. Seamless robes were rare and of great value. The officers agreed to gamble over it later, the robe was abandoned while the soldiers snatched rations of wine, bread, and cheese set out for those ordered on watch.

Abijah first spied his donkey grazing in a thicket. Nearby he saw his friends. They were huddled together, arms linked, and heads bowed. He looked around and didn't see Barabbas. The boy whispered, "He said I was to stay with you."

Abijah edged toward the group, lifted the lamb, and gently nestled the young one back into Mary's arms for comfort. He knew and understood her need to cling to life in these moments to come. A grateful look came from Rachel.

The lamb sensed the moment also. Facing Mary, cuddling his front small legs around her shoulders and nuzzling his soft head into the curve of her neck, he closed his eyes to sleep. Mary felt baby breath upon her face, and the tiny heartbeat pulsing her ribs. She had learned to read God's way of talking to, loving, and never leaving her. This was one of those moments. God now com-

44

forted His beloved Mary in what would become not only her greatest pain, but the world's greatest sorrow.

Meanwhile, Barabbas pushed toward Jesus who stood with the guards surrounding Him. For reasons uncertain to him, Barabbas edged toward this man who stole his thoughts the past few hours. As was custom, a priest was allowed contact with a prisoner before being put to death.

Barabbas moved closely as if to council. A guard said, "He hasn't given us any trouble. Go ahead, priest."

The guard stepped away to flirt with a young woman in the crowd who was obviously trying to get his attention.

Head lowered, face hidden, Barabbas moved cautiously and closely to the Nazarene. With his back to the people and guards, he slowly lifted his hood, revealing his battered and bloody face to meet another battered and bloody face. Jesus and Barabbas searched each others eyes for what seemed an eternity. Then quietly Barabbas whispered, "Who are you, Jesus?"

Jesus, even through swollen eyelids and battered lips, beckoned Barrabbas with compassion and hope as He whispered back, "Barabbas—I love and understand you as no other. I am your Good Shepherd. Follow Me."

Barabbas for the first time in his reckless life

felt the most intense emotion of love he had ever experienced. This Jesus knew him intimately, loved him unconditionally, and shared *every* experience with him, be it victory, or defeat. Even now Jesus mirrored his battered self. This truth engulfed him in such ecstasy and light, there were no boundaries, no confinements, only intense freedom.

Barabbas understood. This man's kingdom was not of the Roman Empire, or of revolutions or of worldly things, but the battles of the heart, the unseen, what is beautiful and good, what is sorrow and pain. What is lived, is learned, and is loved. This reality shook Barabbas to the core. His heart propelled him to new understandings of what his life was all about. He stood frozen in time with the Almighty.

When Barabbas returned from his thoughts and looked around, Jesus was being led away.

XI

Drumrolls announced the resuming of the crucifixions. A cheer arose followed by a sudden hush,
with only the wind moaning through caves below.
The executioner, a powerful hulk of a man, stepped
from a shed. Mallet and iron spikes rested in his
hands.

"I bet the Nazarene goes first," wagered a soldier.

Tension gripped the crowd. Abijah's eyes
roamed the oppressive heavens that foretold a
storm. He drew his face closer to his old donkey,
not daring to look to the arena. Nearby Mary stood
trembling, still holding the lamb to her breast, eyes
closed, still praying.

Soldiers, expecting trouble, stood ready. Four
guards dragged Jesus. With quick precision of
having done this skill many times, each man

47

grabbed an arm or leg, lifted Jesus like an animal and slung him onto a crossbeam. The thud shook the ground. Tethered horses nearby bolted, piercing the silence with high-pitched neighs.

As the executioner stepped forward, he raised the mallet. The hammer thudded and thudded again and again. There was not a sound from Jesus nor the crowd.

Meanwhile the other two men to be crucified were readied. The fear and horror in their faces pulsated the crowd's pleasure. Tivon began to heave violently, throwing up on himself. The guard flung him aside, calling for a recruit to take him to the rinsing area. Tivon, too bloody for recognition, was drug through the dirt to rinse off the stench. The crowd loved it and gave a cheer.

Barabbas didn't hesitate his stride toward the rinsing area. Hecklers by the dozen had lined up and crowded around the victim.

The soldiers, having buckets of water lined up on weather-beaten and blood stained wagons for situations such as this, joined in on the fun, but not wanting to get splattered with the vomit and excrement. One officer, greedy with delight, shouted, "For a price, you can drown the bloody thief!"

Coins, flasks, jewelry and other miscellaneous tradeoffs were quickly made while a dozen or so motley looking men grabbed water buckets mak-

48

ing a circle around Tivon. A frenzy of fun followed. Water splashing, laughing, cat calls, and chaos. Clearly, the crowd loved it. Finally three officers, sensing things could get out of hand, silenced the crowd shouting, "That's enough!" They shoved their way in for the prisoner, using swords to back away the hecklers and a mud splattered priest. Tivon, rinsed clean, was then dragged back to the arena, while another commotion was distracting the crowd.

As was custom, the soldiers nailed placards, called titulus or title boards, above the heads of the crucified indicating to the public their criminal act. The one above the first thief plainly stated, "THIEF".

Jesus' title board, the exception of the norm, was written in big capital letters that appeared to be in agitated handwriting with Pontius Pilate's signature at the bottom. Pilot, in his perturbed state, writing it himself, wrote it in three languages so everyone would understand clearly. It said, "THIS IS JESUS OF NAZARETH, THE KING OF THE JEWS."

There was a storm of protest from the Pharisees and Scribes as they rushed forward, fists flailing the air. As was custom, the Priests picked up dust, and poured it over their oiled locks, intoning lamentation and denials. Common people joined in. They yelled, "Change it! Change it! There is a mistake. It should say, 'HE SAYS HE IS THE KING OF THE JEWS.'"

The officers stood their ground, shouting back, "We won't change this one. Pilate has decreed, 'I have written what I have written!'"

Then one officer, covering his hand over his mouth, whispered to the other, "Pilate knew exactly what he was doing. This is his way of getting back at the religious order. Ha! They are furious!"

A scribe, putting on a show for the delighted crowd, in a frenzied state, paced in front of Jesus' cross, ripping his sleeves shouting,

"If He be the King of Israel, let him come down from the cross and we will believe Him."

Another Pharisee shouted, "He boasted He would tear down our temple and raise it in three days. Let Him now restore Himself and we will believe Him."

The crowd joined in the taunting by screaming, "We have no king but Caesar. Hail Caesar! Hail Caesar! Hail Caesar!"

Soldiers pushed in with swords, moving the demonstrators back, quieting down the protestors, and getting on with their assignments.

The crucified bodies were yanked upward and placed upright in the center arena. Young boys, racing forward, dragging heavy pails, poured river gravel into the iron supports. These supports, driven deep into the rock base of the hill, held timbers solid, scarring the shoulder of the sky.

Jesus, arms spread wide, eyes closed, was quiet. The hostile thief on his left, was being heckled by the crowd chorusing, "Baaaaa! Baaaaaa!"

Infuriated, the thief screamed, "You scum! I'd cram those sheep guts down your stinkin' throats if I had the chance."

Abijah jerked his attention to these last comments. Turning to an officer, he asked, "What did he steal?"

"We've been on this wolf's tail for some time. He's been poaching and black marketing sacrificial animals in the area. With the Passover, and an increased demand for sheep blood, he has had a booming business. Caught him two nights ago with a wagon load he tried to ditch into a river when he knew we were closing in on him. Bloodied up the river is what he did, making it unfit for drinking the next week or so. This one's merciless."

Abijah felt his heart racing as he moved under the cross of the first thief. Looking up into the blackened eyes, he wanted to rip them out. The man sneered down at him, then spit into his face.

Abijah's rage overtook him as he paced like a caged animal. All his emotions of desolation, anger, and hatred boiled up. So this was the creature that slaughtered his children. His loved ones. The innocent. The gentle. Taking his staff in his trembling hands, he lifted it high above his head to strike his enemy. Revenge was all he sought. The criminal, blood dripping from his palms, laughed wickedly at the old fool's fury.

As Abijah lifted his eyes, he unexpectedly shifted his hostility to the left, looking straight into the sorrowed face of Jesus, who suddenly spoke out, "Father forgive them for they know not what they do."

Abijah was immediately swept away to the stable many years ago. To that time of radiant joy, the light, the music, and complete innocence. Nothing could ever be so bad on earth that couldn't be overcome by the glory of remembering this. The unconditional love of a babe in the manger. Abijah sank to his knees, sobbing. Within his soul, love battled hatred. He finally made a choice. When Abijah rose he knew he had stepped back from the darker side of himself. Love took over as he shifted his gaze from Jesus, who he knew forgave him, to the thief, to whom he calmly whispered, "I also do likewise and forgive you."

Abijah turned his back to the thief, and walked away.

XII

✤

Jesus hung alone and forsaken against the bosom of the sky, as the mallet echoed the strikes, sending sparks, crucifying Tivon. The rinsing had taken some time out of the schedule, and the soldiers moved as if to beat the storm that brewed on the horizon.

Mary prayed. Still holding the lamb, her eyes remained glued to the face of her son. She was not of this world, but seemed transposed. The others with her were also quietly praying.

Abijah turned abruptly to see Barabbas comforting Elrad at his side. Obviously their plan had fallen through as the soldiers hoisted the last cross up into the skyline. Tivon now joined the crucified, the three bodies suffering in agony, alone and nailed to their crosses.

Gray clouds were moving in and shouldering Mt. Herman like a prayer shawl. The crowd, pleased but tired of the day long circus, began drifting away from the arena. Gusts of wind were driving dirt into their faces. Pulling mantels around flirting eyes for the soldiers, young women skittered away into the distance. Others slowly followed.

Soldiers, their heavy work completed, settled into their groups of guard duty. As flies buzzed around their sweaty beards, they guzzled ale and began their game of knucklebones, gambling off the clothing of the crucified. Suddenly the first man nailed shouted to Jesus, "Aren't you the Christ? Save yourself and us."

Jesus remained still.

The third man nailed turned and rebuked the first, saying, "Don't you fear God since you are under the same sentence? We are punished justly for we are getting what our deeds deserve. But this man has done nothing wrong."

When the third man spoke, Barabbas and Elrad moved to the foot of his cross. Abijah, feeling compassion for them inched beside them putting his arm around each saying, "I'm so sorry Barabbas."

The man's shoulders began to shake with his

hands covering his head, crying. After a moment, the face lifted to the light, and spoke to his brother hanging on the cross. "Why?" he pleaded.

The man on the cross, answered, "Because I love you, my brother."

This thief then turned his head to address Jesus, hanging beside him, "Lord, remember me when you come into your kingdom."

Jesus turned to His comrade saying, "I tell you the truth, today you will be with me in paradise."

The crucified man smiled at Jesus and answered, "I will follow you anywhere, Shepherd."

Abijah's eyes widened as he looked horrified from the man dressed in the priest robe next to him and then to the thief upon the cross.

"Lord have mercy!" he whispered.

Barabbas had taken his brother's place and had just been crucified.

XIII

✿

Cart wheels whined and groaned with soldiers moving and cleaning equipment from the arena. The crosses hovered over them as they silhouetted against the darkened sky. Abijah embraced Tivon, who was very shaken at seeing his brother.

"What happened?" Abijah whispered.

Tivon spoke as if catching his breath between short sobs. "It all happened so fast. After being taken to the rinsing area, there was a frenzy of men dousing me with water, a lot of commotion. The next thing I knew, Barabbas was yanking me up, throwing this robe around me, and shoving me into the fracas of men. I heard his men arguing with him saying, 'This isn't how we planned it. Are you sure you want it this way?'"

"Barabbas commanded back, 'This is the only way! Otherwise you all will eventually be rooted out and crucified. Our work is done here. I have no family, but my brother does, and so do many of you. Go back to them. This will end my quarrel with Rome, for Rome will never find the great Barabbas. My revolution is now to join this man, Jesus. To follow the example He sets. I believe great changes of the human heart will come from this day. I'm glad to be a part of it. Now go!'

"Barabbas flung himself to the ground, sloshed in the mud, and raised his arms in the battle gesture of slamming the right fist forward and then slap-clasping that wrist with the left hand. The men responded in same manner. Before I knew it, I was here and he was there."

Tivon, arms around his son, afraid to let him go, shook his head in disbelief.

"It all happened so fast."

Tivon slowly moved his eyes to his brother's face. He knew him so well. They were twins. Builds, beards, smiles, stances, piercing blue eyes, brown curly hair. Identical in every way, but temperament. Tivon meek and mild, Barabbas courageous and strong.

Tivon admired his brother. Barabbas never turned away from a challenge or fear. He stood his ground when making up his mind about something, embracing life rather than cowering from it. And there he was defying the pain and anguish, almost reveling in the adventure. Barabbas kept his eyes on Jesus until his final breath. His last words were, "Lead me, and I will follow."

Tivon told Abijah to pass the word along to the soldiers that the family would come and claim the body later. All that were crucified had to have the bodies removed by the families or the body would be tossed to a rubbish heap and burnt.

Storm clouds gathered like hungry hornets as Tivon and his son trudged down the hillside to gather with the lost and bereft men of Barabbas. Finally the revolutionary group dispersed and set to return home to their families, beginning new direction, beginning new ties. Only the courage, love, and unselfish commitments of Barabbas remained strong within them.

XIV

Mary was cold. Even though she moved from the shadow of the cross into the sunlight, no heat could be felt. Only the lamb saved her from shaking, giving her his warmth, penetrating the void inside. She sunk to a kneeling and wailing position expected of women in the face of death. Other family members and friends were already wailing and weeping. Only John, one of Jesus' disciples and best friend stood close by her side.

Mary bowed her head.

"What am I to do now Lord?" she prayed.

All her life, Mary had a strong will when it came to embracing God. Her soul magnified Him in all she did. Now she wondered how God could be glorified in this moment of sorrow. In her unique experiences with Him she knew in all things she was to give thanks. As hard as it was to accept this crucifixion, she did just that. Her understanding of this horrible scene being played out before her was not justifiable to her reasoning. But Mary moved herself beyond the consciousness of her mind and handed the agony back to Her Creator, Her Friend, Her Love, Her Spirit, Her God. In this moment of appreciation for the bigger picture of life, she knew that God was using this stage to not only take man's pain, sorrow, and death upon Himself, but to reassure all His children that death was only a stepping stone back to the place of belonging.

"Lord, if this be Your will, I will give anything, even my own Child, if it brings You to glory. I don't understand, but I lay this burden at your feet. I am one of your lambs. I will follow you even into the valley of death with my Son. I fear nothing when you are with me. Your rod and your staff comfort me. The torrent waters of my soul are stilled when I am with You. Thanks be to You oh Lord. Amen."

Mary, rising, stepped forward and gently laid the lamb at the foot of the cross. The lamb, so small, so innocent, lay content. The gesture was all she could do.

Jesus opened His bruised and blood-caked eyelids and intently studied Mary and John, whom He both dearly loved. He said, "Mother, here is your son."

"John, here is your mother."

In the face of death, Jesus still had concern for His mother. Mary's household was now without a man's protection. Jesus, as was custom, was assigning Mary to be placed in the care of John's family.

How hard it was for Jesus to give up His mother, His teacher, His friend, His earthly flesh and blood. Their relationship from now on would never be the same. Jesus would go on, become all knowing, to dance and sing with the unchained spirits of heaven. Mary would be left behind to carry on until her day to pass over. Each understood their loss.

John put his arm around Mary and walked her back into the shade near Abijah. The heat was getting unbearable, and the storm clouds were pressing down upon the hill.

Mary couldn't look skyward much longer. Jesus was suffering. As a boy He was hurt very little. Few accidents. Few cuts, bruises, or broken bones. He once confided to her that he knew He was going to endure great suffering one day saying, "When that day comes, mother, please try and understand that I need to experience this pain and sorrow. I can't do that in heaven, because in heaven there is only joy and love. A candle can't glow in the sunlight. It only gives light against the blackness of night. So weep not for me when I go through the storm, for the great rainbow of My Father's love will follow. And because of the valley, the mountain heights will be that more glorious."

Mary savored the memory of these words.

Just as suddenly, her heart was pierced as Jesus' eyes roved the crowd, searching for something calling out, "I thirst."

A sponge, soaked in vinegar and pushed between the forked ends of a long branch, was raised to His blistered lips and swollen tongue. He refused to drink the bitterness. Mary knew it wasn't water He cried out for. He used water and drinking often in His preaching as an allegory of faith. Thirsting is wanting and Jesus wanted to return to the bosom of what all humans long for. To return to the origin of love. To return to the great embrace of God. To return to the satisfaction of the soul. He thirsted to get there.

Mary wreathed her hands to know her Son was so close, yet so far from His destiny. She felt helpless, knowing mothers can do nothing as they watch their children struggle in the face of life's challenges. Her voice was trapped in her chest as she pleaded, *"Why can't I help my son?"*

God intervened in her mind, *"Because each and every soul I place on earth has lessons to learn, and experiences to live in order for their spirits to grow. They find out who they are and what they are capable of becoming. In the final hour of all lessons, be it joy, success, conflict, despair, or sorrow, the soul and I are alone. Face to face. Many turn away from me. And there lays the raw fear and loneliness. For those that call upon me, My help, My answers, My celebrations and My support comes in millions of forms. Each and every spirit I place upon this earth is my own. My love. My greatest creation. My perfection. Everyone counts, no matter how sick, how disfigured, how ignorant, or how lost. I love each soul intimately but often differently. Do you think I would create anything less, my dear Mary? Yes, Jesus is struggling. He is experiencing the dark hour of man.*

Jesus lifted his eyes to the heavens and cried out from the cross, "Eloi, Eloi, lama sabachthani?" Which means, "My God, my God, why have you forsaken me?"

" Mary, don't worry. Everything is fine. I am with Him. I am with you all . . . even through death. And always."

Jesus heaved His chest upward, threw His head backwards, and opened His eyes wide. A light streamed down from the heavens. Bathed in gold,

His holy spirit tugged away from His battered gray body, and with great joy, His soul sprung forth into exhilarated freedom.

So light, so beautiful, so translucent, ascending through portals of mystical sunbeams surrounded by millions of archangels, heralding trumpets. The heavenly choirs echoed alleluias throughout the universe, the golden city of human souls stood breathless, and great anticipation pulsated the heartbeat of the Kingdom.

Jesus journeyed triumphantly to the throne of God, straight into dazzling glory, surrounded by brilliant hues of rainbows, straight into the warm embrace of His Heavenly Father.

This moment in time splashed divine love on all life, be it heaven or earth, binding us all together forever.

In the crossing over, Jesus' spirit joyously shouted out for all the universe to hear,

"It is finished!"

Mary, the mother, heard God's proud echo in her heart, *"Well done! Welcome home, My Son!"*

XV

Abijah felt the oppressive stillness as the executioner approached the crucified bodies. Carrying the death lance, lips laid back in an ugly grin, he boasted, "Death is no less death if it comes swiftly with mercy. I am the merciful." Turning to the few scattered observers around the arena, he took a bow and laughed.

The Jews did not want the crucified left on the crosses during the Sabbath. In order to hurry the deaths, the Romans considered the leg-breaking and lance thrust a merciful death compared to letting them hang for days.

Like Hades' impatient heart in the underworld, the morbid man's rough hands slipped a cold iron bar behind Barabbas' legs and cracked the bones. Although already dead, his body slumped leaving his face still turned toward Jesus. The executioner stopped for a moment and studied the man. Shrugging his shoulders he said, "I don't understand that one. He looks peaceful."

Stepping over to the other thief, and with a grin, he once again took the cold bar and cracked the legs. It dropped the body, collapsing the lungs. The thief fluttered his eyes backward into his head and mumbled his last curse. The soldier laughed saying, "No one has claimed you. You will be hauled to the valley of Gehenna, sprinkled with lime, and left to rot. Better yet, they may throw you on the refuse fires."

The executioner walked over and studied Jesus. Seeing no life, he quickly lifted his lance and thrust it beneath the ribs and into the heart, thus fulfilling the prophecy that claimed "not one of His bones would be broken," The act, known as perforatio, brought a sudden flow of blood and water pouring in colored cascades, splashing down on the executioner's breastplate.

The executioner jumped back, staggering, clawing his uniform where he was drenched in blood and water. In all his years of crucifying, he had never seen blood and water pour out separately, the red so vibrant, and the water so pure, shimmering mystically side by side, but not mix-

66

ing. It beaded up with crystals of light, pulsing and glistening with some irresistible force. Staring as if a dead man had risen, he screamed, "Surely He is the Son of God!"

Pulling out the lance, He ran away shouting the same over and over. This last act was the final blow releasing the wind's of God's pain for man's deeds, and as a result, nature's fist pounded the table of earth. Darkness was flung around Golgatha like a black cloak, as she trembled. Long low rolls of thunder roared a warning. Two soldiers, playing knucklebones, gambling over Jesus' purple robe, watched the top of the rock jiggle their stones. It heaved upward and began to split. Horrified, they flung the robe and ran. The robe, carried by the cold wind, landed encircling the lamb at the foot of the cross.

Mary, Abijah, John, and Rachel stood motionless as Mary Magdalene led the other women away, running for safety. Lightning, like silver thread, wove in and out among them. Only the dead bodies of the three crucified hung silently against the black sky.

Mary too felt the ground rumbling. Her feet moved as though she were sliding in mud. Her hands grappled the air as the ground under her heaved up, raising her to Abijah's height. Looking into his face, both of their eyes widened with fear. Large drops of rain splattered the stones.

Faster and harder the rain came. The wind shoved and pushed. John grabbed Mary's elbow, "We have to leave!"

Torn with decision, Mary's gulped a response, "We can't leave Him alone."

John looked at Abijah as rain began pelting, slashing, and stinging. Behind them a lightning bolt seem to rip the covering off the sky. A cypress tree behind them split in half and the acrid smell burned their nostrils.

Mary pointed to the lamb standing alone, shaking, lost, and crying. John swiftly swept him up in the purple robe. His muscular arms cradled the small life that looked lost in the sea of wet purple.

By now those still left on the hill, including soldiers and a handful of people, were running and screaming in every direction. One scribe in particular was on his hands and knees scratching at the mud, nails breaking, and wailing into the gale over and over,

"Surely this was a righteous man. Oh God! What have We done?"

The earth, shaking beneath him, suddenly cracked open swallowing him in a gapping hole, an abyss that lay open a slit in Gogatha's skull. A sour stench of rot issued from the gap in the ground like the reek of a dead carcass. Into this yawning mouth toppled trees, boulders, and bushes.

A low rumble rose to a terrifying roar as half

the solid ground near the cross of the first thief pulled away. The beam, barely holding the body, teetered undecidedly, then collapsed and disappeared into the deep hole. The other two crosses remained steady against the darkness.

The grasping fingers of the storm tore the roof off a shed, picking up the walls and rolling them like empty caskets against a boulder, smashing and spraying the splinters into the belly of the wind. Mary gathered her skirt, and with her wet garments sticking against her, she looked at the others calling into the wind, "All right, let's go."

Abijah, horrified, tried to stand but fell back, unbalanced by the sickening sway. He tried again and managed to pull himself up by the side of his donkey, standing unsteadily, afraid to take a step. He grabbed onto Rachel who also was trying to steady herself.

John, holding his balance with the frightened lamb, managed to lay it across the donkey's withers. Then quickly adjusting the wet robe as a padding he lifted Mary up. Placing Rachel behind her, he prayed the donkey could manage under the strain. Grabbing the bridle and throwing a steady arm around Abijah, he tugged the burdened donkey forward, shouting, "I know where to go if we can make it."

Mary looked back at Jesus swaying in the storm but she was quickly spun about as the wind seemed to lift the donkey up and shove them on. Her mind churned and tightened into a knot as fear brushed the edge of her mind. She was always strong in the presence of Jesus. Always in control. Always assured. Now He was gone from her side. This storm was swallowing her world and everything that gave her life meaning. Only the lamb at her side kept her countenance as she gripped the curly wool in her wet hands. She didn't know if the scream ringing in her ears was her own, or the thunderous roar of rending rock about her.

Rachel hugged her closely from behind, whispering in her ear, "It's going to be all right, Mary. Hold on."

Like a man possessed of unknown strength, John led the group clambering over and around boulders bouncing and rocks sliding. Although it was late afternoon, the convulsed land shook in the blackness of night. John could not see where he was going, but followed his instincts, half running and winding down the hillside that brought broken cliff ledges bouncing around them on both sides.

The donkey kept up a steady trot, snorting and wheezing in the excitement, his sides steaming with heat. Often his back legs buckled under the burden or slid down in the mud. The women clung solidly. John's steady arms kept tight control and kept them all moving through the maze of destruction.

Mary and Rachel felt as if their bones were being jiggled loose. Mary struggled to keep the lamb from sliding off. Leaning forward into the wool, her tears flowed and her heart fluttered like a wounded bird.

"Now, my Son. Now! I am afraid. Help us."

They fled the base of the crucifixion hill, being dragged through bushes that tore at their clothing. Winding their way into an opening of a rock formation, an alcove tucked under a sand mound, they stopped abruptly in the dark.

Panting, dripping, and sweating, they felt the sudden calm and security of the solid rock surrounding them. Outside it sounded as though the earth choked and gasped, sending lightning that seemed to crack the walls of heaven, followed by deafening thunder. Like a hand spanking a stubborn child, the gales brought branches, trees, and anything loose, bashing the firmament outside where moaning, crying, and wailing was heard in the distances of nowhere.

Groping to connect with one another, John helped Mary and Rachel down, all sinking to the ground, resting in quiet fear. Listening. Wondering. *What happened to their world?*

XVI

A chill permeated Mary's wet clothing, deepening her despair. Numbness overtook her spirits as she and the others sat quietly listening to the dreaded sounds outside.

When she lost her husband Joseph to death, she was surrounded by family, friends, and community. It was a difficult and lonely time, but the strength came from the ongoing normality in her home and community that surrounded her. She took up with doing and giving, knowing Joseph's spirit was always near. His soft laughter that she loved so much, she often found tucked into the sounds of daily chores. Eventually she found herself able to go on without him. She continued to grow and become an independent woman. She walked more solidly with her God. She spent more time tutoring, listening, and spending quality time raising her Son, Jesus. But this! Taking her Son from her in the midst of such a confused and upheaveled world was a difficult trial for anyone, even a chosen one of God.

She did what her heart lead her to do. She took hold of Rachel's and John's hands. Abijah joined the circle of support. The gesture brought warmth and comfort within the walls of aloneness and sorrow. Mary began softly as the others joined in the Psalm 23:

"The Lord is my shepherd, I shall not want.
He makes me lie down in green pastures,
He leads me beside still waters.
He restores my soul.
He guides me in the paths of righteousness
     for his name's sake.
Even though I walk through the valley of the
     shadow of death.
I will fear no evil.
For He is with me.
His rod and staff comfort me.
He prepares a table before me,
In the presence of my enemies.
He anoints my head with oil.
My cup overflows.

Surely goodness and mercy will follow me all
the days of my life.
And I will dwell in the house of the Lord for
ever."*

They sat quietly in the dark contemplating the words of hope. Finally, Abijah pushed his aching bones up groping his way to the donkey. Finding his lantern, he lit it, placing it upon the ground. A small hole of radiance illuminated the black cave causing shadows to dance upon the walls.

No one moved except for the lamb, now inside the circle, stretching his legs and sniffing the sandy soil. Knowing lambs as he did, Abijah began what he called the shepherd's coo or the calling of new life. Pulling out his olive branch flute from his baggy pants, he wet his lips, smoothed down his beard, and began to play a popular shepherd's tune.

Hearing the high notes, the lamb began to frolic, kicking his heels, pouncing and bouncing. Shadows moved upon the walls as if God's hand was erasing a blackboard of doubt upon the hearts within, replacing it with the spirit of trust. Momentarily Mary was divided. She was pulled down with the pain of the day, but was lifted up with the joy of watching the lamb.

Rachel began talking first, "I remember when Jesus was about five years old. He came running

74

into my kitchen saying, 'Look Grandmother! Watch me be a lamb.' He frolicked over my stools, crouched around my cooking pots, and finally hopped onto a wooden box. Then He jumped into my arms, gave me a big grin and hug, and shouted, 'Baaah!' We both laughed and laughed. Such joy. Such trust. Such big beautiful eyes like this lamb's."

Rachel turned to Mary, "Mary, share your favorite story."

Mary took a deep breath, giving it some time. "He was around fourteen years old. He didn't come home for dinner. After fretting a few hours, I was about to go searching. Finally Jesus came in carrying a wounded lamb. The lamb had fallen into an old abandoned well. Jesus said that He lowered Himself with a rope, making a sling for the injured animal and hoisted it up the side of the wall to safety. He said any lamb lost, no matter how far it goes, or how hurt it may be is worth saving.

"I knew the slum area well and wondered how Jesus managed the climb. The picture I have left in my memory is a young man, muddy hair sticking straight up, scratches from head to toe, tunic torn, carrying a frightened lamb with a splintered leg. He handed me the most victorious grin I have ever seen." Everyone smiled.

John then joined in, "He talked about sheep

so much in His teachings, that we disciples had this wool robe made by the finest weavers in Rome. There aren't many like them and they are extremely valuable and of the highest quality. No seams. It was a great gift for Him. It served as warmth from a chill, a protector from the sun, a blanket to sit on while teaching, a towel after dips in a river, and a pillow under the stars. John stopped to slowly trace the outline of a fish in the sand. Then said as if mostly to himself, "I shall write this all down someday."

Mary picked up the robe and held it gently to her face, breathing in the scent. Just at that moment, the lamb stopped, stood still, tensed up his legs, stiffened his tail, and let out a long baahing cry. Abijah laughed saying, "That's hunger."

Rachel rose and checked the gourd hanging on the donkey. There was a little goat's milk left in it. Abijah took off his scarf, tied it into a knot and dipped it into the milk. Forcing the wetness into the mouth, the lamb suckled hungrily for the nourishment in the cloth. After getting the hang of it, his little tail fluttered like butterfly wings. Abijah pointed, "There's the sure tail sign of satisfaction."

All laughing, Mary then took the makeshift nurser and continued feeding. A gentle smile came to her lips. She spoke softly, "Just when you lose everything that is precious to you, and your world crumbles in the brink of the storm, hope comes in the form of new life and new love."

Finishing the feeding, the lamb yawned. Mary lifted him into her arms, once again to feel the love of a baby, the soft breath of God.

Nibbling on the turnips handed out by Rachel, the women finally nestled down upon Jesus' robe, exhaustion and sleep taking them over. As the storm continued howling and cursing outside, the friends slept safely inside a cocoon of grace.

XVII

Lightening flickered through the entrance of the cave as they one by one arose. It was predawn and the storm had subsided. John spoke.

"We must get back to the hill to claim the body. Yesterday Joseph of Arimathea, a good friend of Jesus, got permission from Pilate to take the body and bury it in his own tomb. Since Joseph is a wealthy man and a member of the Prominent Council, Pilate agreed, but only when his guards reported back to him that the body is dead. Pilate is planning to roll a huge stone in front of the tomb, placing guards on watch. He wants to make sure nothing unusual happens with this burial. Nevertheless, I am suppose to meet Joseph this morning to help take Jesus down."

"We'll leave with you," said Rachel, "and gather with the women to prepare for the burial. We will need spices, perfume, and linen cloth for the anointing and wrapping of the body."

Mary gathered her skirts, shaking out the sand saying, "Today is the Sabbath and according to the commandments, we can't dress the body until tomorrow. We will go home, see what is left of the village after this storm, prepare the spices, and meet you at the tomb. Following this storm, we may have other bodies to prepare."

Rachel faced her, "Do you want to take charge of the anointing, or do you want me to? Will you be all right?"

Mary took a deep breath, "My mother always said when sorrow overtakes a woman, she still has her work to do. The pain doesn't go away, but the beckoning chores are God's way of helping her work off the anger and restlessness. I want to get back helping. I want to keep going as Jesus would wish me to do. With time I believe I will be fine. I will get on with life. Right now I will begin with baby steps. Taking each day as God leads. Let's get on with this difficult chore. Yes, I will take charge of my Son's anointing."

Rachel reached for Mary's hand and gave it a supportive squeeze. John picked up the robe and began folding it, getting ready to go.

Packing things on the donkey, Abijah planned

to help in what was needed in the aftermath of the storm. He then noticed that the lamb was gone. Looking around, he couldn't find him.

Mary didn't remember the lamb leaving her side in the night. Everyone began checking over and around the cracks and crevices in the cave. No lamb.

Abijah said, "Please take the donkey and go on ahead. I will stay back and look for the lamb, and will meet you on the hill later."

Since dawn was moving in and the body was to be down, they all agreed. John, Mary, and Rachel moved quickly out of the cave with the donkey. Abijah, keeping the lantern, stayed behind to find the lamb.

The donkey's hooves and the women's voices receded into the morning mist leaving Abijah feeling quietly alone in the dark cave. He shivered. Standing helplessly he thought, *"Where could he have gone?"*

Searching deeper into the walls of the cave, Abijah found a crevice into a black hole. He heard the wind of the subsiding storm crying through the opening. Or was it the wind?

Lifting his lantern, Abijah squeezed himself through the crack. Having trouble with his hearing, he cupped his hand to the blackness within. He heard it. A pitiful cry of the lost lamb that only a shepherd understands.

It came from below. Abijah, taking his shepherd's staff with the hook on one end, hung his lantern on it and lowered it into the deep hole in the floor of the cave. Deeper and deeper he punctured the blackness.

Getting onto his knees and stretching his arm down, he swung the light to and fro searching for the wee small cry. Finally he saw him. Lying on his side, obviously injured by the fall, panting and looking up to the shepherd for help. Heart pounding in his chest, Abijah feared the worst for he couldn't climb the precipice to the bottom.

Frustrated, he sat upon the ledge wondering what to do. Finally he could not wait any longer. If he could get to the small ledge above the lamb, he could reach down and catch the small neck with his staff hook and drag the lamb within reach. He positioned the lantern for light, and lowered his staff, letting it drop to the ledge, echoing lonesome clatter in its fall.

Abijah's unsteady fingers shook as he slowly slid over the edge on his stomach, clutching the rock and kicking sand downward. Legs dangling, he scraped his sandals up and down trying for a foothold. Feeling like his arm sockets would give out, he found a crevice to wedge his toes taking some weight off his arms.

He was spread flat, clutching the face of the rock. Resting for a moment, he could see the small grains of sand sparkling as he stared into the wall. *"Funny,"* He thought, *"How all these tiny grains of sand holding fast together make a solid strong fortress together."*

Then he looked down. Fear gripped him when he realized how far down it was to the ledge. Palms sweating and heart racing, he inched his old body rock by rock down the incline. With a few feet to go, his right arm began to shake violently. So violently that it let go, causing him to slide recklessly over jutted rocks, landing on the ledge. Breathing heavily, he lay prostrate in the sand. His ribs hurt. Further down, he clearly saw his lamb.

Abijah's shepherding skills were acute. He had climbed down rock inclines many times to rescue sheep. All kinds of weather. All kinds of locations. Even in the dark of night. The act was second nature to him. Inside he felt like a young man that could scramble the ledge and bound up the wall with the lamb like a mountain goat. Unfortunately, in reality, his aged body held him back and he was frustrated with his inability to do what he wanted. He wasn't even sure if he could get up.

He decided to remain on his stomach. Groaning, he reached for his staff. Inching it downward with the hook sideways he tried to reach the lamb. It was too short. Sliding on his belly he stretched farther over the edge saying, "Come, little one. I won't leave you. Somehow we'll to make it."

Suddenly the rock ledge gave way with a crash sending Abijah plummeting down in a rock avalanche sliding headlong, sweeping the lamb up against himself. They were pinned against a boulder. Abijah let out a cry as he moved his leg. There was pain is his hip. The scourging from the fall took its toll. Abijah felt the weight of a boulder on him even though there was none.

Gritting his teeth, Abijah pulled himself up into a sitting position, drawing the lamb on his lap. The small one's eyes looked up at him. So innocent. Pleading to be helped. Pleading to understand the pain.

Embracing the baby, and not being able to help the suffering was Abijah's greatest torment. He buried his face in the wool, feeling failure. The shepherd could not help his lamb. He could not lead him to safety. Abijah cried in the darkness as his lamb died in his arms.

XVIII

❁

The lantern, high upon the ledge dimmed, flickered, and finally went out as if a serpent had swallowed the light. Abijah felt layers and layers of suffocating blackness. Terrifying heavy silence.

He waited. No sign of comfort. No ray of light. No sound in the void.

Finally, the old shepherd spoke not in a weak voice, but in a pitiful one like a child locked in a dark closet, "Help me, O Lord."

The words pried open the sealed box of his soul, the light leaking through the cracks. The rays giving hope. Abijah continued speaking, "Lord, I know it's only a small lamb, but he's all I have. He is my child. I don't know what to do. I don't know where to go."

More light squeezed out as he softly said, "It is death that frightens me. I lost my wife, my sheep, and finally my courage with yesterday's crucifixions. I am old and afraid. If you are out there Lord, I need to know before I go into nothingness."

The lid of the soul completely opened revealing an intense light. Abijah was dazzled by the beauty, the light engulfing and illuminating the cave. As he stared both inward and outward, there slowly appeared before him, the figure of Jesus, grand, majestic, and smiling. He stood on the ledge above him wearing a white robe and sandals that shone. He looked as He always had on earth, although enclosed in radiance. There were wounds of blood upon His hands and feet.

Abijah gasped. Jesus was holding his lamb! He looked down at the ashen limp form of the lamb in his lap. How could this be?

"What's the matter, Abijah?" Jesus asked, seemingly amused.

"I'm confused. I've got my lamb. And you've got my lamb. I know it's my lamb because a shepherd knows his sheep. Yesterday you were dead. Now you are standing in front of me. Please explain."

Jesus set the lamb down upon the ledge, letting it hop, frolic, baah, and wiggle its tail. Then turning back to Jesus the lamb lifted his front hooves upon His robe to be picked up again. Jesus lifted the lamb into his arms. Turning to Abijah, he smiled saying, *"Mine has life. Yours has not."*

Abijah's mouth dropped open saying, "I saw him die."

"No Abijah. We are not dead. We just changed forms. Like the butterfly that lifts away from the dead cocoon, our spirits leave our earthly forms behind."

Abijah asked, "How can this be?"

"It is not as difficult as you make it out to be. Watch."

Jesus intensified in light. His body with the lamb began fading until He became hues of an illuminating rainbow.

Abiajh was overcome by the beauty, shielding his eyes, surrounded by the great voice saying, *"I am the Creator. I am Light. I am Goodness. I am Truth. I am the Way. I am the Great Unseen. I am the Alpha and the Omega. I Am. You may have trouble understanding this as will many of My children. Nevertheless I created all things from myself, even my Son Jesus."*

And here the rainbow turned back into Jesus holding the lamb. *"Man relates better to flesh and blood than to an Infinite Creator who has billions of prisms. Trying to figure Me out and know all of Me would be as hard as trying to count the sands of grain on earth.*

"Wanting not to limit myself, and to be able to feel all the emotions of life everywhere and in all time, I placed a small spirit of Myself in every child born on earth. That is how I know and understand each of you intimately. Why I love you all. Why I understand you. Why I am always with you.

"I took on the death experience to show how easy it is to go from one existence to another. And to prove that the spirit I formed inside of you lives on, I am now coming back temporarily to show myself to you and many others and demonstrate that resurrection comes to all My children at death. This transition is always seen as a fearful torment for you . . . but for me it is a celebration."

Abijah sheepishly asked, "How was it?"

"How was what?"

"I saw you suffer. I saw you die."

"Believe me, my dear Abijah, I did feel great pain. I felt sorrow and torment beyond all measure. I took the pain upon Myself because knowing what all of you go through in your earthly experiences, what you endure as My creations, in all circumstances, I love you all the more. I understand. And because I understand, I forgive your weaknesses.

"As I crossed over, everything became far more beautiful than the earthly world. It smelled of true sweetness, and the sounds of pure creation

87

blended every good and beautiful thing with divine love. A misty veil lifted from My eyes. I knew who I was as My spirit and Light came back to join My Father. A homecoming. Where I, and all My children belong . . . together in the light."

Abijah asked, "Why is there so much fear, sorrow, sickness, and pain in life, especially before dying?"

"The time before crossing over quite often is very painful. With some more, others less. Why? Earth is a place of choice. And with choices there are mistakes. Mistakes lead to conflict. Conflict silhouettes the light and darkness, giving light more beauty. Coming from darkness into light lets each spirit see who they really are, what they are capable of enduring. Would I create blessed beauty before coming back to blessed beauty? Of course not. Doesn't a cold drink of water taste so much better after crawling through the desert? Aren't the green hills of home and the loved ones waiting that much more rewarding to the prisoner of war? Thus My reunion of perfect love with My children is that more profound. This is the resurrection gift I freely give to all My children."

Abijah sheepishly asked, "All your children?"

"Yes, all My children."

"Barabbas?"

"By all means, Barabbas. He was a spirit with much courage. We certainly cheered his return."

"What about the other crucified thief?"

"What about him?"

"Where is he?"

"He is with Me also, but in a place of learning."

Abijah looked startled.

"You must remember, Abijah, all souls born to earth are My unique creations. Some choose never to tap into My light of love. Because I allow choice, many choose the darkness. They choose not to make contact with My light buried deep within their souls. Lights not used become embers that smolder the heart. They live a horrible existence while on earth for which when they return to Me, their true selves are recognized and rekindled. This often brings them to sorrow, to forgiveness, or to redemption.

"Because they have erred doesn't mean I love them any less. They come to earth under billions of situations. Some easier. Some more difficult. Would a mother love her child any less if the child broke her favorite vase, or finished last in a race? No. The child is her own, her life's work. She won't give up on him. She believes in him. She loves him more than life itself.

"Man has a narrow picture of love. It's conditional. My love is unconditional. Yes, the thief is home. He is forgiven. All has been revealed to him. I haven't given up on him. There is still work

to be done with him. Eventually his spirit will be true to the light."

All Abijah could say was, "I see."

"Well, Abijah. Are you ready?"

Abijah laid his head back upon the rock. Fluttering like a bird in a cage, his heart swelled gripping his ribs, wanting to fly away, but afraid to leave the protection of the cage that held it captive for so long. It was free to go.

Abijah struggled to breathe and couldn't. Fear and pain tried to grab him back to earthly reality for only a second, but then melted into pure love as he reached out a hand to the Great Shepherd. His spirit triumphantly burst forth and then he broke free. Like the butterfly leaving the cocoon, he lifted up into perfect beauty. With great joy he shouted, "Yes Lord, Lead me home."

POSTSCRIPT

All of heaven rejoiced at bringing Abijah back to the Kingdom of Light. This humble figure of a good and simple man played out his existence on earth caring and tending sheep all his life. He didn't acquire riches of gold, or the conquering of armies, but left a glowing trail of love in small deeds of kindness that rippled into the hearts of those he touched. And it was this path that led him home.

Picking up in the aftermath of the storm, Mary carried on serving the poor, the homeless, and the sick, ministering in her Son's name, and continuing to spread divine love. She earned the titles "God-bearer" or "The One Who Understands The Deepest of Human Sufferings." This extraordinary soul left us all entwined into God's Oneness.

The lamb that was so much a part of Jesus' life and ministry remains with us today. He symbolizes the essence of Jesus, The Good Shepherd, The Lamb of God. This lamb's appearances with Him or representing Him are endless. Wherever you go, in all walks of life, in all places, the lamb reminds us to trust and not be afraid.

And in ending the resurrection story, The Great Shepherd of the Sheep speaks out the simple words of love to those that seek to serve. His words are simply, "Feed My Sheep."

The lovely, the lonely, the lost . . . even to the last lamb.